Last to survive

Chapter one

In 1907 lived a small village within the Woodsedge Forest. The forest was beautiful as a forest should be, filled with wild trees, flowers and animals alike. The trees stood tall and green as they have for centuries before, the flowers grew lush and with an array of different colours producing the loveliest of smells. The village that lived within this forest was filled with the happiest of people who lead simple lives, they did not care for luxuries or for power. For the people that resided in this village had a task that was bestowed on them centuries ago by the most powerful of magical beings, four sorcerers all of which held the abilities to control one of the four elements; Earth, Fire, Water and Air. As they grew in age and with no successors born to carry on their legacy, they created a way to preserve their magic.

The four sorcerers travelled deep into the woods to a stream by a bridge built with the wood of the healthy oak trees nearby. The trees by the stream spread their branches wides above the river, the bright green leaves blowing gently in the breeze.

Last to survive

The river that flowed through the forest was clear and beautiful, the river ran so clear that you could see the riverbed below that was filled with enchanted rocks that could retain magical abilities. Each sorcerer plucked a stone from the river and travelled back to the village in the dead of night. The following night with just them and an entrusted young teenage boy they went to the village temple. In the temple, the stones that were plucked from the river were placed on a alter in an underground room of the temple. The sorcerers performed the spell to transfer the magical abilities of the elements to the stones, the magic whirled around in different colours around the room before falling into the stones. Each stone glowed in colours that represented the ability it now possessed; green for earth, red for fire, blue for water and yellow for air.

They explained to the young boy that if an evil being ever come after the stones. He is to take them back to the River throw them in and recreate the spell they gave him on a single piece of parchment, completing this task will hide the stones until the next lot of successors arrives in Woodsedge. The young boy promised that he would guard the stones with his life, no evil being would ever have the stones in their possessions.

Last to survive

That young boy had since died within the last century so passed the task down through the generations of his family. A young man now held the job to protect the stones. Within the last few months, the village became aware of a man who went by the name of Ubel, he was sorcerer but one that searched for power and luxuries. He had heard of the capabilities, of the four stones, and he wanted that power. Ubel tried to find where the stones were kept, but he was unsuccessful for no one apart from one knew where the stones resided, and no one in the village knew who the one person was for all of their own protection. Ubel offered riches for the stones hoping that the village would accept this generous offer, but they declined. Ubel went back to his cave in the depths of the forest filled with rage. If he could not bribe the village to give over to stones, then he shall take them for his own. Over the next few months, the village grew in numbers after a message was sent out asking for other villages to connect with them to protect the element stones from the evil clutches of Ubel.

One fateful night in the year 1908 Ubel rose his army of loggerheads. An army that lived for nothing but to follow orders from their master, they didn't think for themselves, they were like

Last to survive

fleshy robots, brainwashed to do his dirty work. One dark night Ubel ordered his army to attack the Woodsedge village, they marched into the village and invaded homes and burning the buildings, while some villagers fleeing with children others stayed to try and fight the loggerheads. Still, it was hopeless, with Ubel's magic powering against them the loggerheads killed those who chose to cross their path. Once the village was nothing but ashes Ubel walked over towards the temple, as he reached the temple, it was searched high and low, but no stones were found. All that was left was an empty podium... the stones had gone. Ubel screamed with anger, someone had got to the stones before he could, why did he not see this coming?

Meanwhile, running through the forest towards the river was a young man. His families promise to the four old sorcerers all those years ago to protect the stones no matter what the cost. This man did not have a wife or children, so is the last of their bloodlines. Like Ubel, this young man was a sorcerer, it was a gift bestowed by the four old sorcerers onto his family in return for protecting the stones. He did not care for the power these stones held, he simply cared to live in peace. The young man reached the river and got the four

Last to survive

stones out, throwing them in the river he recreated the spell given to his family;

Do not resurface

Till you sense for hearts with purpose

Come and break the spell

Then protect them from the immortelle

Stay under for a century today

Then show your energy

Once the chosen four, appear

Only then will the charms reappear

He watched as the stone's glowed as they fell through the clear water and into the river bed the colours disappeared, and the forest was silent. The footsteps of the loggerheads could be heard getting closer. The young man fled from the river into the night.

Last to survive

<u>100 years later</u>

It's 2008, and Woodsedge village was now a much bigger community, on the outskirts of a big city. In place of the village was a community with hundreds of houses and a big Academy at the very top. Woodsedge Academy was big and modern, almost like a museum from the outside and they pride themselves in having the most educated and wholesome students that always aimed high. Each student that entered this academy had talent of some sort. In the playground of this Academy on a cold winter morning was around 200 kids running around, chatting, passing notes and laughing. The bell rang, and the students all filed into the big Academy until there was nothing but a few dead leaves blowing across the playground.

In an English classroom sat a young girl at a desk with long brown hair, bright green eyes and light freckles across her nose and cheeks. Her uniform was clean and neat, her school tie was tied correctly, and her blazer and school shirts were neat and clean with a small shiny badge pinned on labelled 'School council.' This young girl goes by the name of Sophie, she's only in the lower years but is one of the academy's model students,

Last to survive

straight A's and loads extracurricular clubs, she especially did dance and gymnastics. Her class was studying Romeo and Juliet.

 "Now can anyone tell me the true meaning in Shakespeare's play Romeo and Juliet?", asked the teacher. The young girl put her hand up; the teacher points to the young girl allowing her to speak.

"It's about the hatred of two families, the true meaning behind the play is a lesson in prejudices because of the families being prejudiced against each other which then ends in the death of Romeo and Juliet". The young girl answered confidently.

"Well done Sophie. That's correct", Sophie smiled and continued with her school work.

As we travel through the Academy into the science block, we can see two young boys in their class, but unlike the other students, they were not paying attention. Instead, these two were talking to each other unaware they had been caught by the teacher.

"I cannot wait for lunchtime," said Jake. He was tapping his pen on his school book with one hand

Last to survive

and leaning on the desk with the other hand fiddling with his dark blonde hair.

"I know the sooner this lesson with Mrs Bord is over the better," answered Justin. He was also leant on the desk with one of his arms, his longish brown hair intertwining with his fingers. Every so often he looks up at the clock to check the time, as he looked up again and he saw a very stern looking middle-aged lady with grey roots and glasses on a gold chain.

"Having a nice chat over here boys?", asked Mrs Bord, making Jake jump and both the boys sit up straight.

"Ummmm... yeah we're just saying how interesting your lesson is Mrs Bord.", Justin answered hoping to get them both out of trouble, while she stood in front of the boys with her arms crossed. The boys lowered their heads, they knew that they were in trouble and in the academy getting into trouble in class meant one thing... Detention. Mrs Bord sighed turned round and started walking back towards the front of the class, as she turned round behind her desk, she addressed them in front of the whole class.

"Maybe then you two boys would like to review the notes of my lesson in detention after school!"

Last to survive

The whole class giggled and tutted as the boys leant back on their desk.

In the academy's sports hall, there is a class playing football. One young boy in particular was moving very fast through his classmates. Andrew was very good at sports he played in most of the matches when the academy had house tournaments, as he scored a goal and ran the opposite way one of the other boys in his class stuck their leg out sending Andrew across the floor. As the rest of the class laughed Andrew stood back up, he pushed this other young lad.

"What's your game ben?" Andrew shouted as Ben stumbled backwards.

"Temper temper Andrew." said Ben as he caught his balance and approached Andrew again with his mates following behind. "Maybe it's about time your girlfriend learnt a bit of first aid? She could spend the lunch hour patching you up when we're done."

As Ben and his friends gathered around Andrew, the teacher blew the whistle before they got the chance to start fighting.

Last to survive

"That's enough! To the changing rooms everyone!", The class all ran off towards the doors. Andrew went to leave the hall when the teacher stopped him.

"Not you Andrew. I want a word with you." Andrew sighed and knew what was coming, he knew he shouldn't have reacted the way he did.

"Yes sir.", Andrew turned round to his PE teacher who was standing with his arms crossed.

"Now Andrew you're a talented lad when it comes to sports but your temper lets you down now you know as well as I do the rules at the academy so you will have detention today after school." Andrew sighed

"But Ben started it sir! He tripped me on purpose."

"Well unfortunately I didn't see him. I only saw you pushing him nearly to the ground so after school today Andrew, report to detention." The teacher left the hall and Andrew followed on to get changed ready for the lunch bell. As he got changed and slipped his blazer on, he turned round to the mirrors to fix his tie and tidied up his messy light brown hair out of the way of his green eyes, just as he picked up his bag the school bell

Last to survive

rang for lunch and he rushed out of the changing rooms.

In the playground by the trees Sophie was stood looking at the Phone with her bag on her shoulder and her coat folded over.

"Hey Babe!" Sophie looked up and saw Andrew walking towards her, she smiled and put her phone into her pocket.

"Hi! how was class?" Andrew sighed

"I got detention after school." Sophie widened her eyes

"Detention? What for?" Andrew scratched his head; he knew that Sophie wasn't going to be happy that he almost got into a fight.

"I nearly got into a fight but I didn't start it, honest! Ben tripped me up during class." Sophie sighed; she didn't like Andrew getting in fights but she did have to admit to herself that Ben has got it coming to him so wasn't surprised that they nearly got into a fight. Just then Jake and Justin came over to the young couple.

"Guess who just got detention from Mrs Bord miserable old cow.", said Justin, Sophie giggled

Last to survive

"I swear you three might as well just live here." Justin looked confused as they walked over the lunch hall.

"Hold up what do you mean three?" asked Jake. They were all waiting in the lunch hall in the que to the food.

"Oh, you didn't know Andrew landed himself a detention as well." Justin and Jake giggled while Andrew couldn't help but smile.

"Yeah one more moment and Ben would have been on the floor."

"Got into another fight then eh cuz." Said Justin through his giggles.

They all got their lunches and went to sit down at one of the tables. They had a pleasant lunch hour talking about the rest of their classes. Although they were all in different years these four in particular had a stronger bond of friendship; Justin and Jake had been best friends for years and were in the same year at school, they didn't always get into trouble because they did enjoy some lessons for example I.T. When it came to technology Jake and Justin were the people to ask. Justin and Andrew are cousins and then there

Last to survive

was Sophie, who was friends with Jake and Justin but she was also Andrew's girlfriend. They all lived within a minute of each other in Woodsedge so were always together in and out of school, when the boys weren't in detention.

"Well I've had gym practice after school tonight so I will still be here when you three have finished serving your time." Sophie laughed as she took a drink from her water.

"Yeah, yeah but that's cool we will come up to the hall after then." said Andrew. Sophie was particularly good at gymnastics and was in the academy's gym team, when the contest was at Woodsedge then the boys would go and watch her compete.

Later on, in the day the boys had just left detention and made their way to the sports hall where Sophie has her Gymnastics practice. When they arrive in the hall, they sit themselves down behind the barriers where Sophie had her bags placed, Sophie was on the big gym mat and just landed from a double black flip. Sophie ran over to her bag and Andrew passed over her water bottle, as she took a swig the boys noticed a girl that they hadn't seen before.

Last to survive

"Hey Soph, who's that?", asked Justin. Sophie turned round to look at the girl Justin was referring too.

"Oh! That's Beth, she is playing catch up. She's from the other academy across town, she missed her practice because she was on holiday so her parents paid for a catch-up session over here. To be honest she is a bit of a snob. Thinks that she's so entitled."

They hear the whistle from the gymnastic coach and Sophie runs back over to the centre of the hall.

A few moments later the four friends were leaving the academy. It was cold and flakes of snow were beginning to fall as they walked home for the night. It was a happy life in school in their little bubble. Sometimes things at home though weren't as perfect as they seemed.

Now it's not to say that any of these for four young people were abused or starved, but like every child, they all had their own events going on at home. Jake came from quite a typical family; his mum was the type of lady to welcome anyone with open arms into her home. A lot of days after school it was the place the gang would

Last to survive

hang out when it got too dark, because Sophie and Andrew were still so young their parents preferred for them to be in a house when it's dark and then be dropped home safely after. Justin and Andrews' family were a middle-class family, they all lived on the posher part of Woodsedge. Sometimes Justin and Andrew would be dragged to family events at a moment's notice, and sometimes they didn't even want to go. Still, they didn't have much choice, they had a big family. Hence, it was customary to go to a lot of events.

Being Andrew's girlfriend, sometimes Sophie would go to the more local family gatherings, but it wasn't very often. Sophie was barely at home; she had a lot of extracurricular activities at school. There was a reason for this, Sophie's mum and stepdad didn't earn very much and what they earned went away on bills and basic food before they could even see it. Sophie's mum worked a lot of hours so was at home late a lot evening, and her stepdad worked part-time and prefers Sophie to be out of the way. A few weeks ago, Jake's mum offered to look after Sophie a few evenings in the week so that her stepdad could find a second job, Sophie's mum took the offer. Things were a little easier for Sophie's family because they knew that she was being looked

Last to survive

after. Sophie's real dad wasn't around much, mostly because he was also in poverty. Her real dad did some time in prison, not for anything majorly dangerous, he wasn't a murderer or anything like that, but he wasn't exactly a role model in his community. Sophie's real dad did pop up from time to time, but it wasn't very often, the last time was just before she started senior school.

Chapter two

On the weekend our four friends were walking through Woodsedge on their way to the shops. They had decided to take a walk down into the forest so stopped off to get some drinks and snacks. There weren't very many shops in Woodsedge, a lot of the residents have to either drive or get the bus to the main town in order to do their big shops. The nearest shop to them was owned by a miserable old man who didn't like the youth in Woodsedge and watches each one like a hawke whenever they are in the shop.

In the shop owner's defence, there was some of the youth in Woodsedge that liked to terrorise and bully people for a hobby, one of the people in this 'gang' was Andrews bully at school. They were the type of people you didn't want to be associated with, because of their actions most of the community did not approve of the younger generation, even some of the parents. Sophie, Justin, Jake and Andrew were all used to the comments they would get walking around the community. They were even used to being watched by the old shopkeeper as they went in to get drinks and snacks on the weekends.

Last to survive

The four friends were in the shop at the back of the aisle picking their drinks from the fridge, the old shopkeeper was watching them from behind the counter over his thick glasses that were perched on his nose. They just ignored the shopkeeper and paid for their things before they left to set off for the forest.

For winter Woodsedge was clear and sunny, but it was still cold enough for people to be wearing their hats and scarfs. Every so often flakes of snow would fall from the sky and brushes off of the orange and red leaves still on the trees. The four friends made their way through the forest to the old bridge by the local river. Even though it was winter the forest remained just as beautiful with the leaves changing from green to orange and red, one by one the leaves slowly fell from the branches to the forest floor below. The river had a thin layer of clear ice over the top of the water's surface, you can still see the water running underneath. The four friends make their way over the bridge to the clearing by the river, they got out some blankets from their backpacks and set them down on the forest floor, leaves crunching under their feet.

Last to survive

For the next few hours, they had fun chatting and messing around, they came down to the forest quite often because it was away from Woodsedge. Away from parents and teachers and nosey old shopkeepers, just them and the beautiful nature around them. They liked being around nature more than hanging around the local parks and the community centre, it was more peaceful and they always wondered what it was like to live in Woodsedge years before the community was built. As the boys were climbing the trees Sophie had a book in hand.

"Oh, Sophie has a book in her hand surprise." The boys did tease Sophie about her love for reading but they never meant anything by it, they actually respected her thirst for knowledge and stories. Sophie was brought up to focus on her studies, this was something both her mum and birth dad agreed on because both of them didn't do well at school so wanted better for their daughter. Andrew jumped down from the tree and held his hand out to his young girlfriend, "Come on Soph, come and have some fun, if I know you that book will be finished by tonight." Sophie smiled; she knew that Andrew was right. Sophie stood up and they all spent the next hour having fun climbing the trees.

Last to survive

As they were climbing down Andrew turned and saw something in the river.

"Hey guys look in the river." The other three looked to wear Andrew was pointing, from under the ice something was glowing brightly. They all went down to the edge of the river and looked closer to discover there were four stones in the riverbed glowing different colours.

"Shall we get them out?" asked Sophie, they looked round for something to break the ice with. Justin found a small but thick branch and they went back to the river and tapped gently on the ice as the cracks formed and the ice break away the stones started to glow even more and they also started shaking all on their own. The four friends stubbled back with shock at what they just saw. As they stepped back, they all tripped and landed on the forest floor, the four stones jumped out of the water on their own and landed in front of each of them.

"What in the world just happened?" Jake said, finally breaking the silence. The three boys looked at Sophie.

"Don't look at me, I don't have a clue, I'm just as confused as you three." It was a habit of the three boys to look in Sophie's direction when they didn't know what was happening or needed

Last to survive

information, which happened to be quite often. They all slowly moved closer to the stones and then picked them up. Standing up they were all trying to figure out what they were; Were they toys that were dropped by some kids? How were they glowing?

They decide to take a stone home each and then in the morning go to school and see what they could find out. They packed up their blankets and made their way back up to Woodsedge.

Sophie walked though her front door and her dog Pippa greeted her as she took her coat, hat and scarf off. She pulled the bright green stone from her pocket and looked over it to make sure it wasn't damaged. Mark, Sophie's stepdad, was sitting in the lounge and noticed what Sophie had in her hand.

"What's that in your hand Sophie?" This came as shock to Sophie because her stepdad didn't pay much attention to what she did unless her mum had forced him.

"Ummm... it's a stone. We found four of them down in the river in the forest earlier." Mark got

Last to survive

out of his chair to look more closely at the stone in his stepdaughter's hand, his eyes widened and he hid a smile from Sophie.

"Well you better put it somewhere safe then, hadn't you?" Sophie went up the stairs. Mark smiled as he heard her bedroom door close. "Because you never know whose hands, they may end up in."

Later on, that night Sophie was reading in bed when there was a knock at the door.

"Come in." her door opened and her mum walked in.

"Hello dear, how was your day then?"

"Oh, me and the boys went down to the forest and we found some weird stones in the river so we're gunna take them to school tomorrow and see what we can find out about them."

"Where is the stone you have then?" Sophie pointed over to her desk, her mum walked over and picked up the stone, looking at it in her hand she walked over and sat on the edge of her daughter's bed.

Last to survive

"Wow it reminds me of the Woodsedge legend." Sophie stopped reading her book and looked up at her mum.

"What legend?"

"I'm surprised you haven't heard it at school, It's said that years ago when there was just a small village living here there was four stones that held the powers of the elements well there was an evil sorcerer that tried to get hold of them but they were then hidden away until the next four people who were destined to control the stones appear." Sophie's eyes widened, was this one of the stones from the legend?

"Anyway, you need to get some sleep for school tomorrow." Sophie's mum placed the stone on her daughter's bedside table and then kissed her goodnight before leaving the room switching the light off. Sophie turned over and went to sleep.

During the late hours of the night all of the four friends were asleep each stone started to glow and shake on their bedsides, then from each stone a small burst of magic energy appeared in a colour to represent the four elements; Green for earth, Red for fire, Blue for water and Yellow for air. Each burst of magic slowly landed into each of

Last to survive

the four young teens in their beds. As the magic absorbed in their bodies, they each started to briefly glow in the colour of their element.

At the same time elsewhere deep in the forest Mark walked through the forest under the darkness of the night, with only the moonlight and stars above him. He had a dazed look around him almost as if he was in a trace, he then reached a cave in the depths of the forest and briefly stood at the entrance before walking into the blanket of the shadows in the cave. A few moments later a loud, spine chilling scream could be heard echoing from the cave, the sky went from clear and bright to dark and cloudy. Clashes of thunder swept the night sky while bolts of lightning flashed over the forest, as an evil laughter came from the cave the collapsed body of Mark plummeted to the ground. Another man walked out with a clean looking wooden staff in his hands with a black glass ball on the top, the man himself was tall and pale in complexion but had dark hair and piercing orange eyes. He wore a cloaked black outfit and as he stretched out his hand a clap of thunder rang across Woodsedge.

In the community all four of the young teens were woken by the thunder, thinking nothing of it. They went back to sleep in their beds, ready for school the next morning.

Last to survive

Elsewhere deep in the forest the mysterious man was now standing in front of the most gruesome looking crowd of people. He then addressed the crowd.

"AFTER A CENTURY OF WAITING OUR TIME FOR REVENGE AND POWER IS UPON US, LOGGERHEADS THE STONES HAVE APPEARED AND SHOWN THEMSELVES AT LAST AND NOW WE HAVE OUT CHANCE TO TAKE THE POWER OF THE CHARM ELEMENTS ONCE AND FOR ALL."

The crowd of Loggerheads started to cheer and chant as the man smiled with ecstasy, his time for revenge had come.

"UBEL UBEL UBEL." The dark sorcerer silenced his army,

"WE MUST HOWEVER HAVE PATIENCE MY LOYAL ONES FOR I HAVE A PLAN FOR OUR NEW CONTROLLERS OF THE CHARMS, THEY ARE NOTHING BUT CHILDREN AND WILL NOT TAKE LONG TO CRACK, THEN MY FRIENDS, THEN WE CAN TAKE OVER ONCE THOSE BRATS ARE OUT OF THE WAY."

There was another roaring cheer and chanting, the thunder and lightning storm continued across

Last to survive

Woodsedge as Ubel and his army went back into hiding for now until the plan could be put into action.

Chapter three

The next morning, the sudden overnight thunder storm wasn't the only news buzzing through the houses. Sophie and her mum had woken up that morning to find that Mark wasn't there, no note was left behind. After asking around, someone saw Mark walking out of the house late at night. Sophie's mum asked Jake's mum to look after Sophie that evening. After saying goodbye to her daughter, she rushes off to look for her husband. Sophie and Jake then have some breakfast and go off to meet Justin and Andrew. While on their way to school Sophie told the boys about the story that her mum had told her the night before.

"So, you think that this story is real, that legend has been told for years and there's no proof it ever happened." Justin took a look at his blue stone in his hand.

"But there's no proof it didn't happen either." Sophie has been thinking about it all morning while having her breakfast, her and Jake had even spoken about it.

"Sophie has a point Justin. How can you explain that those stones jumped out of the water all on

Last to survive

their own?" After thinking about it himself Jake had to admit that it was very strange.

"Why do we go and ask the head of History at school? He's a local man he's bound to know about the legend and whether there's any proof of its real or not." suggested Andrew. The other three teens agree that this is a good idea and carry on to school, although little did, they know their school day wasn't going to be as normal as they were expecting.

Later on, at school Sophie was in her PE lesson, usually she can pay attention to every but I seem to be different she couldn't get the stones off of her mind. Thankfully today in her year was cross-country day, so what she was doing was running around the school on her reign of time to think about the legend and if anything, that's been happening made any sense. as Sophie was mid run, another girl in her class tripped her over sending Sophie plummeting to the ground, the rest of the class couldn't help but giggle.

"Being Petty again Alix? Don't you have anything better to do?" Alix, a tall girl in Sophie's year walked up to the young girl and she towered over her.

Last to survive

"I was hoping you could put that brain box of yours to good use and do some homework for us." Sophie got up and brushed herself off.

"Why don't you do it yourself instead of getting behind the bike sheds." The whole class gathered around Sophie and Alix.

"You will regret saying that!" Alix made her way towards Sophie fists clenched when they heard a cracking above them, as Alix and Sophie looked up a tree branch that had broken off and was coming hurtling down. Everyone moved quickly out of the way, the branch narrowly missed Alix. The teacher ran up to the class and blew the whistle for everyone to go back to the changing rooms, as everyone else left the teacher went up to Sophie.

"Are you okay Sophie? Do you need to go to the school nurse? That branch was rather big." Sophie shook her head, as the teacher made their way back to the school Sophie turned round to look back at the tree with the fallen branch.

"It's almost as if the branch purposely missed me." Sophie said to herself before running back into the school to get changed. As she went past the art block she waved to Jake and Justin who were inside having their art lesson.

Last to survive

In the Art classroom Justin and Jake's class were doing still-life painting. Justin was leant on the table with one hand while rinsing his paintbrush in the jar of water in front of him, he watched as the blue paint exploded into the water. When he lifted the brush out, he noticed that the water was starting to spin around quickly and slowly forming in the middle was a gap that was increasing as the water moved. Justin's eyes widened and tapped Jakes arm, as he looked round to the jar Jake also saw the water moving.

"What in the…" Just before Jake could finish his sentence one of the boys in their class through a piece of paper across the classroom which landed in front of them. Jake blew it out of the way, as he did the windows opened with a strong gust of wind and the vase the class was painted flew off of its stand making the whole class jump from their chairs, including Justin and Jake.

"Alright everyone, no need to panic, it's only some broken crockery, everyone back to your seats." The teacher then went to find a brush to sweep up the mess.

"Here Jake you don't think…" The boys looked at each other.

Last to survive

"The stones are doing this; the legend must be true." They both looked at the broken vase as it was being swept up. Did they cause the vase to break?

In the science block Andrew was in a class watching a demonstration. Ben was sat behind Andrew trying to taunt him and get a reaction, he tapped him on the shoulder then leant forward

"Here I dunno why you're paying attention, doesn't your brainiac girlfriend do your homework for you?"

"Shove off Ben at least I have a girlfriend." As Andrew turned around Ben scowled at him.

"Yeah you do, properly through pity though, can't see it lasting long." Andrew started to grip his pen more. He was trying to focus on the demonstration, Andrew had remembered that he promised Sophie he wouldn't get into any fights in class. As he was focusing on the demonstration the metal being held over the bunsen burner suddenly got engulfed in the flame, so much so that the science teacher had to quickly dunk it in the water nearby. The smoke from the water rose to the ceiling of the classroom and through into the hallway, the school fire alarm started ringing loudly through the whole academy.

"Right everyone to the front of the Academy!" Andrews class filed out of the science block along with the rest of the academy making their way through the grounds to the front playground area.

About 20 mins went by and everyone was waiting in their classes to make sure everyone was out of the building and that there wasn't any fire. Andrew looked to his left where Sophie was lined up with her class and she smiled at him.

"Do you know what set off the fire alarm this time?"

"It was my science class. The bunsen burner went mad." The principal then stood on the top of the hill at the front of the playground with a megaphone.

"OKAY EVERYONE QUIET PLEASE... THANK YOU, NOW BECAUSE OF THE TIMING OF THIS FIRE ALARM WE HAVE DECIDED TO LET YOU ALL HAVE AN EXTRA 15 MINS OF LUNCH BREAK YOU MAY ALL CARRY ON OUT HERE AND PLEASE WAIT 10 MINS BEFORE HEADING TO THE LUNCH HALL." The principal went inside and all the students went off to find their friends. Four students in particular were eager to find each other, they wanted to know if anything had happened in the other classes. Sophie and Andrew found Jake and Justin at the back of the playground.

"Hey you two did anything weird happen in your class today?" Sophie and Andrew looked at each other, Jake had taken the word right from their mouths.

"Yeah."

"Yes."

They were all starting to be convinced that the Woodsedge legend was true, that it wasn't just a wife's tale passed through generations.

"We need to find Mr Legna if anyone will know where we can find proof it will be him." Sophie pointed out. The other three agreed with Sophie, they needed to find out more about the legend and where to find more information about it. They all headed up to the history block and to the end classroom.

As they entered the classroom they looked around, Mr Legna always had an immaculately clean and decorated classroom. He had a colourful timeline through history all around the room, at the back of the classroom was a little

Last to survive

library with any history book you needed to do your school work and to the left of the little library was a desk packed with supplies the students could borrow if they couldn't afford their own. Mr Legna walked in and saw the four friends.

"Ah Justin, Jake, Andrew and of course Sophie what can I do for you four?" They suddenly didn't know what to say, they knew what they wanted to know but how do they put it to their teacher without sounding like they had lost their minds.

"We were hoping that we could pick your brain about something sir." Sophie told him politely.

"Pick away kids picks away." Mr Legna turned round and started writing on the bord for the next lesson. Justin cleared his throat before speaking.

"We were wondering if you knew anything about the Woodsedge legend." Mr Legna stopped writing and turned to look at his four students. Everyone had heard of the legend but never has he been asked about the legend; he looked more closely and saw the slight glow in each of their pockets.

"Ummm well how much do you all know about the legend." Mr Legna leant on the front of his desk as Sophie explained what her mother had told her last night.

"Well it seems that Sophie's mum has covered the basics, and there is no evidence it ever did happened but then also there's no evidence it didn't either... if I were you four I would keep an open mind about it, if such stone do appear then I will say this for the people they present to.. It will be a battle for survival the evil sorcerer who was known as Ubel has wanted these stones for over one hundred years... another point to the legend is that there is a book that only presents itself to the chosen four when it is required and its said to appear in this academies library as this used to be the grounds of where the original sorcerers who controlled the stones and its powers or the elements."

"So, what elements do these stones control?" Andrew asked.

"Earth, fire, water and air, the four main elements of this world and together were told to have immense power." The four-friend looked shocked.

"Tell me you four, is there any particular reason you are asking so many questions about the legend?" They all looked at each other and

Last to survive

silently decided not to say anything about the stones just yet until they knew more.

"No sir we were just curious to see if there was anything more to the story that's all." Sophie said before they left the classroom, Mr Legna sat back down at his desk.

"You kids will soon find out what will happen, I have to keep my eye on them from now on."

Last to survive

Chapter four

The rest of the school day seemed like it was going backwards, none of the four friends could concentrate in their class, not even Sophie. Did they really hold the stones to the elements? Is that why all those weird things had been happening? Each of them watched the clock as it slowly ticked to 3pm, Home time.

The three boys had to wait for half an hour on the school steps waiting for Sophie, it was Monday which was when the school council met. Eventually Sophie emerged from the building.

"Hey Soph, how was the school council meeting?" Justin asked while getting up off the steps with the other two boys.

"Oh, you know the same old thing." The boys chuckled.

"So boring then.", Sophie could help but laugh. Even though she enjoyed being on the school council but it could be a little boring sometimes. They start to make their way home, Sophie and Andrew hand in hand and Justin and Jake just behind them pretend to wind them up. For a few minutes they forgot about the weird thing

Last to survive

happening in Woodsedge, it was like before when they didn't have the stones.

"So, Sophie have you heard anything about your stepdad?" Andrew asked his girlfriend who shook her head and explained that her mum did call but to say that the entire area had been searched but he was nowhere to be found. They all decided to sit in one of the local parks around by the swings for a while, Sophie was glad because she didn't want to go home while her Stepdad was still missing. Jake decided to change the subject back to the legend to try and keep Sophie mind off of her missing stepdad.

"So, what are gunna do about these stones?" Jake took his bright yellow stone out of his pocket.

"We need to find the evidence it happened in the first place but Mr Legna said there wasn't evidence either way." Justin pointed out; Andrew then looked up from his own stone.

"No evidence cuz? Sophie's bully nearly gets hit by a tree, you manage to move water and blow a heavy vase over and I nearly set my teacher on fire none of this happened before."

The other three had to agree with Andrew, even though they could all have been genuine accidents, the fact they happened after they stones was too much of a coincidence to ignore. They talked about their next move on finding out more information,

"What about the museum in town, if there is such a famous legend there is bound to be something in there." Sophie suggested but the older two shook their heads.

"Nah we have been there recently on a school trip remember that Jake, there wasn't anything about the legend there."

As they were talking about the legend the sky started going dark, this was odd for 4 o'clock in the afternoon. As the four friends looked up to the sky the ground started shaking and the wind started howling through Woodsedge at high speeds, knocking the teens off of their feet.

"Quick under the dome!" Jake shouted and they all ran to the dome shaped climbing frame; it would at least protect them from any flying debris already running through the paths and across the green into the roads. They all were sat on the floor covering their faces from the dust and small bits flying from the ground. As they looked through their blazers, they saw trees bent over and debris smashing into windows of the houses, they could hear screaming all around them and people shouting to run or hide. The whole area

Last to survive

went pitch black for a few minutes as the ground started to shake fiercely, as the shaking stopped so did the wind… everything went quiet.

It was a few moments before the four teens looked out from under the climbing frame. Everything was still and deadly quiet, they came out from under the frame one by one and looked around at the damage to the community. They decided to get back to Jake's house as it was the nearest and the safest bet if the wind and ground started up again. As they walked through the community, they saw all the blown off doors, smashed windows with falling trees and tipped over cars. One thing they did notice is that there was'nt a single person around apart from them, they found this odd because when they were hiding, they could hear people shouting and screaming. They all entered Jake's house and went to sit in the kitchen, Jake went upstairs to see if his parents were in but they also were nowhere to be seen.

"Where is everyone?" asked Sophie as Jake came downstairs. No one had an answer because they were all just as confused. When they looked on their phones there was no signal, Jake switched on the TV and all they saw was snow on the screen, they tried the radio and there was nothing. The four friends started to worry, no one around and all technology wasn't working, they all decided to go to each of their homes to get changed out of their uniforms and then go back up to the school and while they were doing this, they looked out for any sign of anyone else in Woodsedge.

They made it back up to the Academy and looked up at the massive building, it wasn't bright and welcoming but dark and mysterious. They remember what their teacher said about the site the academy was built on, it was where the original sorcerers for the elements lived, that's if the legend is believed to be true.

"Are we the only ones here?" Andrew asked, again no one had an answer. They did know but they didn't want it to be true... they were the only ones left. But why?

Last to survive

Chapter five

They walked through their school but it was barely recognisable being so dark, it looked as if no one had set foot in the place for years but they only left a few hours ago. Sophie looked in the direction of the library, she then remembered that a certain item would appear when needed.

"Hey I think we should go to the library." The boys looked round.

"Soph now ain't the time to get your latest page turner." Jake said and Sophie gave the boys a look.

"Don't you remember what Mr Legna said... A book is told to appear when needed." The other three remembered and agreed with Sophie.

"Well let's face it being the only people or come to that the only living things in Woodsedge I think would suggest needing that book." Andrew explained.

They decided that the older boys would go and look around the academy for any other clues to what had happened and Andrew would go with Sophie to the Academies library and see if they can find this book, they agreed to meet back in one hour.

Jake and Justin were looking round the back of the Academy's assembly hall, they were on the stage behind the drawn red velvet curtain. Justin started whispering to Jake,

"Do you reckon Sophie and Andrew are alright?"

"Yeah course I wouldn't want to make Sophie mad would you." They both smiled as they carried on looking.

"Nah I suppose not."

"Justin why are we whispering?" Justin stood up straight for a second.

"You know what I don't know were the only ones here ain't we." Again, they both laughed, they then heard the door open and they both went quiet and stayed still as they listened out to see if it was Sophie and Andrew. The voices they heard were not familiar to them, they listened into the conversation,

"Where shall we find these brats then sir?"

Last to survive

"We won't need to log brain they will come to us; they are kids they will come back to their school eventually."

"When they do sir."

"When they do that when we will give them an alternative, give up the stones or stay trapped here forever."

"Why not just destroy them?"

"It's too easy and I will do it but only when they are begging for it... and being children that will not take long, then they will be found to be killed in the freak storm that hit Woodsedge."

Jake and Justin looked at each other, eyes wide; they rushed towards the library to warn the other two.

Sophie and Andrew were looking in the library, they didn't know what they were looking for but they assumed that they would know when they saw it.

"If the book has been here the whole time how have you not seen it before?" Andrew asked as Sophie looked through the bottom shelf.

Last to survive

"I don't know I've read nearly every book in this library and never come across one about the legend."

"I suppose if all of this legend is based on magic the book will be as well"

"Yeah your right." They looked round to the back of the library. There was a glowing light as they reached the back of the room. They saw a book one the floor, it looked old and tattered and they were afraid to pick it up in case they broke it.

Sophie knelt down and gently picked it up, as she opened it, they heard the door open and Jake's voice.

"Andrew! Sophie!" They emerged from the back of the library and saw the older two with shock on their faces.

"What's wrong?" Sophie asked as she put the book in her bag, it was only a small bag but as she put the book in it shrunk itself down to fit inside.

"That evil sorcerer part is true and he is after us, we think he has trapped us here on our own to get the stones!"

"Oh no, where is he?" Andrew asked.

Last to survive

"Here at the academy he knew we would come back here so we need to get out now!" Justin said and then they left the library and went rushing down the corridors. They knew they could'nt leave the normal way because that will be most likely where this evil sorcerer is, they ran down the steps of the science block and went round the building before running across the playground. They reach the side entrance to the school and slip through the gate before running away from the academy.

They kept running past all of their houses, knowing that right now being in a house would be a bad idea, they went to the one other place they knew like the back of their hands... the forest. As they reached the familiar bridge where they first discovered the stones they finally stopped. They were all panting and sweating as the adrenaline slowed down in their bodies, they all sat down leaning on the trees around them.

"Please...say...you...two...found...the...book...that's...meant...to...appear?" Jake asked between breaths. Sophie caught her breath before answering.

"Yes, we did." Sophie pulled the book from her bag, set it down on the forest floor as the boys gathered round her and the book. Sophie opened the book and began to read the text inside,

"If you have found this book then you must be the new chosen keepers of the stone, if you are extremely young or old, we apologize. This book will contain everything you need to know about what happened over 100 years ago in Woodsedge. You will already have your possessions a stone each, these are the element charms, they hold the power to control each of the elements. The green charm controls earth, the red one controls fire, the blue one controls water and finally the yellow one controls air. Unfortunately, magic chooses the keeper so if the charms have appeared to you then you are chosen and this is will carry on throughout your life and bloodlines."

They look at each other, the legend is true, they hold the element charms and the powers that are within them.

"So, who do you think put us in this situation? This evil sorcerer or someone else?" Andrew decided to say this because it's what everyone was thinking. Justin shook his head.

"No, it's definitely this sorcerer we overheard him remember." They knew they couldn't go back to the Academy because that's where he was

Last to survive

waiting for them, that's where he thinks they will go. Jake then suggests something dangerous but sensible if they were to survive.

"We need to go and get some supplies if we are hiding out here in the forest."

"Surely we can't just hide in the forest forever, this isn't going away." Sophie said.

"Yes, but we don't know how to use these powers, what we are even up against for all we know he has an army with him we need to make as much time as we can to learn what we can."

The other three agree with Jake, they need to know exactly what they are doing to control these element powers and somehow try to find out more about this evil sorcerer. They find a safe place to hide the book and then they make their way up to Woodsedge, they go to Justin's house, Justin had mentioned in the past that his mum keeps all the family camping things in their attic.

They entered Justin's house and managed to get everything they could from the attic and food they needed from the kitchen. They got back to their spot in the forest and set down everything, they were shocked that they got out without having any trouble. Maybe this sorcerer is waiting for something, but what?

Last to survive

They go back up to Woodsedge and head to the community centre, as they go to head into the centre building, they hear something behind them. As they turned around there were at least 20 gruesome looking human-like creatures with blunt expressions, they were all staring at the teens as if they were food. At one point the four friends thought they were going to be eaten right there and then. They then heard an evil laugh, as they looked above the creatures in front of them, a man stood on the top step into the community centre area and he held his hands up.

"Well well well what do we have here...children the charms choose children to keep them. It's almost too easy... give over the charms and I will put your beloved community back to how it was." The teens looked at each other and all shook their heads.

"We may not know much about you yet but we know you want these for power... to take over so we know that promise is fake!" Ubel frowned and as his staff appeared, he banged it on the ground knocking the four teens to the floor onto their knees, his loggerhead holding the teens down as Ubel made his way down the steps while the teens tried to break free.

Last to survive

"I am Ubel and I know you will have heard the legendary story of the element charms but till now I bet you thought it was just a fairy-tale, well I can tell you it's not. I will give four kids a straight choice hand over the charms now or stay here till you can destroy me or until I destroy you."

None of the teens said a word, this angered Ubel, back in his time children were a lot easier to scare but clearly in the 21st century they were a lot tougher.

"I see you are not making things easy for me, but remember this... I do not lose to children." With that final statement Ubel and his loggerheads disappeared into thin air. The teens get up,

"Is everyone okay?" Justin asked, everyone nodded and they decided to get what they needed from the community centre then made their way back to where they were camping out in the forest, making sure that Ubel or any of his loggerheads were following them. When it comes to late at night, they decide that while two of them sleep the other two will watch out for Ubel and his army of loggerheads. The older two tell Sophie and Andrew to get some rest, as Sophie and Andrew were sleeping Jake and Justin, for the first time in their lives have serious conversation without one joke insight,

Last to survive

"How long do you reckon we will be here for?" Jake asked his best friend.

"By what Ubel said earlier either until we can destroy him or until he kills us." The two boys looked round at the younger two sleeping.

"They are too young to have to do this, why couldn't these charms wait till they were older? I mean Andrew isn't even 13 yet and Sophie is only just turned it."

"Remember what Sophie read in that book, the magic doesn't see age only the qualities of the keepers."

"Yeah but what are they then like Ubel said we are just children." Justin lowered his head, Jake turned to his best mate.

"Look we must have been chosen for some reason and we will find out how not only for us and to get back home but for Sophie and Andrew like you said they are too young to go through this."

Last to survive

Chapter six

The teen had counted the days they were in the forest, 14 days of no sign of Ubel or his loggerheads. They didn't know why but they were thankful for whatever was keeping him away, it has given them time to look more into the legend and learn how to harness the power within the charms. The older two boys managed to harness their Water and air powers pretty quickly, Justin could not only make water appear from nowhere but he could manipulate water to his will whereas Jake could summon twisters and move or knock anything down using the wind. Sophie took a little longer to harness her powers for earth, for a few days she could maybe make some small flowers appear but eventually she could manipulate plants around her to do whatever she needs or wants. Andrew was having trouble harnessing his fire power, he managed a fireball once but it got out of control and nearly set a nearby tree on fire, Justin had to put it out with his water powers and Sophie fixed the tree before the smoke was seen by anyone.

Last to survive

Later on, that night Sophie noticed that Andrew was sitting away from them trying to produce even a small fireball. She walked up quietly to her boyfriend, Sophie knew he was having a hard time with his charm and until they all harnessed them, they couldn't access any other powers. This was something they had read about in the book, once they all had harnessed the powers from the Charms, together they were able to use other magic enabling them to stand a chance against Ubel.

"Are you okay Andrew?" He jumped at Sophie's voice and turned around.

"Yeah course I am." Sophie watched as Andrew was playing with the forest floor with his trainers, she sighed.

"You are a really bad liar you know, that right?" Andrew smirked slightly while still looking down.

"Why can't I harness my charm yet?" Sophie didn't have an answer, it was baffling all of them.

"Come back and get some rest then we can try and find out why." After a few minutes Andrew agreed to come back to the camp they had set up, since she had harnessed her power Sophie had manipulated the tree to cover them so they couldn't be seen or found.

Last to survive

The boys were finishing some food off while Sophie was reading the legend book and she suddenly let out a gasp making the boys jump.

"What's wrong Sophie?" Jake asked. After a few moments Sophie answered, still shocked at what she just read.

"Back when Woodsedge was just a village there was a young sorcerer trusted to protect the charms and it's said that just like Ubel he also hid until they revealed themselves again to the new keepers." Sophie turned the book around and there was a picture of the sorcerer that protects the charms, it was someone they knew and trusted… It was their history teacher. The boys' faces dropped. That's how he knew so much about the legend because he was part of it, it also explained why he knew so much about history as he lived through it all. Andrew then thought of something disturbing,

"Ummm if that guy has been hiding by being our history teacher then how was Ubel hiding all this time?" The other three thought about it, surely, they would remember a man as creepy as Ubel around Woodsedge. So, the only other way he could was by disguise, but what kind of disguise?

"Maybe he can hide in others, you know in their bodies." said Justin

"That's awful." Sophie remarked

"Well he is meant to be evil Sophie."

"Oh yeah." They figured that he must have jumped from body to body and it had to have been a bloodline in the area. Then Jake thought of someone but he really didn't want to say who he had in mind; it was the one person that went missing after they found the charms.

"Umm I really don't want to put this in your head Sophie but what if he was hiding in your Stepdad."

There were a few moments of silence, Sophie's face dropped. She didn't want to admit that it could be true but it very well could be. She thought back to when she got home after they found the charms, she had never known her stepdad to be so interested in what she did with her friends. The more she thought about it the more it made sense,

"So did my stepdad ever actually exist or do you think it was just Ubel the whole time?"

Last to survive

"Nah I think he just hid in his body until he needed to come back out." Then Sophie sat up suddenly.

"What if Mark is here too!" The boys agreed, surely Ubel would have kept his disguise in where he could keep an eye on him. They decided to keep an eye out for Mark but the real way to save him was to beat and destroy Ubel.

They thought back to the other Sorcerer or as they knew him Mr Legna, Sophie looked at the page and noticed there was a small paragraph by the photo.

"Call on the charm protector, we are in need, to know some of the legends deed." Once Sophie had finished reading the words out loud there was a small gust of wind and the leaves picked themselves up off the floor and spiralled in one space in front of the now scared teens.

"I told you reading is dangerous, Sophie, what did you read?" Shouted Justin over the wind, the teens covered their eyes. As the wind stopped the teens turned round and they saw, standing in front of them was Mr Legna, he looked at the teens.

Last to survive

"Well what can I do for you four now?" Mr Legna smiled and crossed his arms

"How did you get here?" Sophie exclaimed; Mr Legna chuckled. They were confused at their teacher's reaction, what was so funny? They thought that they were the only ones here.

"Allow me to explain, when Sophie read the sentences by my picture that summoned me to you, usually it's when you need me the most so I was waiting for the first call to be honest."

"I think Mr Legna you have a lot of explaining to do." The history teacher looked at the four teens and sighed as he sat down in front of them.

"Let me say first I was really hoping that the charms would not pick people as young as you four, well we might as well start at the beginning so you are fully informed." The four friends settled themselves down and looked eagerly at their teacher as he told them of the day that the village he lived in was invaded and burned to the ground, he described when he hid the charms in the river that the teens found them in, when Mr Legna is finished with his tale Andrew had another question that was playing on his mind.

Last to survive

"Mr Legna you said that you were hoping that the charms didn't pick people as young as us, why is that?"

"Well usually the older you are the more power you can manage to control."

"So, I haven't been able to control my charm at the moment no matter how hard I try." Mr Legna looked confused,

"How old are you Andrew?"

"I'm 12."

"I see and when do you turn 13?"

"Not for another 2 weeks."

"So, as you have properly already discovered the charms do not choose based on age even though there is an age that in my day you would have to wait till you turned 13 years old until you could do any sort of magic."

The other three looked at Andrew, for at least another 2 weeks Andrew wouldn't be able to control his charm fully or at all, this meant that they wouldn't be getting back to normal any time soon. Andrew started to get upset with himself, he got up and went off on his own. When the

Last to survive

others tried to follow him, Mr Legna stopped them.

"No let him calm down first then go after him, anyway you're trapped here till you defeat Ubel so he can't get very far."

Last to survive

Chapter seven

Under the night sky Andrew was walking through Woodsedge, head to the ground, not even looking out for Loggerheads or Ubel. He got to the park where they were when they got trapped here, he entered the park and sat on the swing. As he sat there, he couldn't help but think that he is the reason that they cannot get any closer to destroying Ubel and getting back to their normal lives. He knew deep down that it's no one's fault, Mr Legna explained that Magic doesn't know the age of the person it chooses. Even knowing this though Andrew couldn't help but feel guilty for keeping the other three here, all because he really was still just a kid, a child, he wasn't yet 13. He knew that this meant that for the next two weeks the other three will have to protect him until he can harness his charm, this thought did not make him feel any better.

Across the Woodsedge Justin, Jake and Sophie are looking for Andrew. They were worried about him, Ubel could be anywhere and Andrew can't defend himself right now if he was to be attacked. Woodsedge might be a small community but it

Last to survive

spread across a vast area so it can take up to an hour to walk from one end to the other, a few hours went by and there was no sign of Andrew. They wondered where Andrew would have gone.

Back in the park Andrew was still sat on the swings,

"I suppose I'd better find the others before a certain sorcerer finds me." Andrew gets up off the swing as he walks across the park, he hears breathing behind him, Andrew slowly turns around and sees three Loggerheads looking back at him. "Oh no not these idiots again." Andrew got himself ready to fight off the Loggerheads. "Our master has demanded your presence boy!"

"Demand? bit rude, sorry I'm a little busy right now." After Andrew spoke the Loggerheads go to attack Andrew. Andrew fought off the Loggerheads for what felt like a good hour before he started to get tired. "I can't wait for my birthday." Andrew kicked one of the Loggerheads right into their stomach knocking them to the ground.

On the other side of Woodsedge Justin's phone rings, they looked very confused but when he

Last to survive

looked it was Andrew! Justin immediately picked up.

"Andrew, where are you?"

"At the park and I'm outnumbered here got three of those Loggerheads on my back."

"Were on our way cuz." Once Justin had hung up the other three start to run towards the park, in the school however they were being watched by Ubel,

"So, they think they can save the baby of the group, let's delay them a little bit." Just as the older three are round the corner a group of Loggerheads appear in front of them making them stop in their tracks.

"So much for this being easy."

"Wishful thinking there Sophie."

"Come one let's get them, then we can get to Andrew." As the other three started to fight off the group of Loggerheads by them Andrew was still going after now 2 hours and he was feeling so tired.

Andrew could feel that his muscles were screaming but the adrenaline was keeping him going, but he didn't know how long for. Andrew was hoping that the Loggerheads would give up before his body did, he knew the others were one their way so he needed to keep going till then.

But after a few minutes more of fighting the Loggerhead managed to get hold of Andrew, as he was trying to break free, they disappeared out of thin air. At the same time the Loggerhead that were holding up the other three also disappeared.

"Where did they go?" Sophie asked.

"I got a feeling they were delaying us." At Jake's thought they then carried on to the park as fast as they could, when they arrived at the park it was empty, they were too late, Andrew had gone. Sophie spotted something by the slide, she went over and picked it up. The boys looked at her.

"What is it Sophie?" Sophie turned round with a red stone in her hand.

"It's Andrew's Charm, he didn't leave willingly he was taken." Fear set over the other three, did Ubel get one of them already?

Last to survive

Back at the academy Andrew wakes up and finds himself in a dark room, as he looks around, he can just about see that he was in the sports hall but when he tried to move, he couldn't. When Andrew looked down, he was bound to the chair, the more he struggled to get free the tighter he was held down. As he looked up to Ubel standing in front of him, he had an evil grin on his face and started laughing, the laugh ran a chill through Andrews' whole body. Andrew had what Mr Legna had told them in his mind, knowing this set fear in his mind. What was going to happen to him?

"Well I've got one already, I knew this would be too easy against children."

"You haven't won yet Ubel!"

"Oh, but I will do by the end of the night, the other three will if they care about you that much give over the charms to save their friend."

Andrews eyes widened; he was the bait for a trap to get the others. His mind was racing with different thoughts and the other three dead because he went off on his own was not a thought, he wanted but it was in the front of his mind, they could end up dead because of him. Ubel then tried to get information out of Andrew.

Last to survive

"So where are the others hiding?" Andrew didn't say anything, he wasn't going to give up their hiding place even if it did cost him his life. They may find it harder but he would rather die so they can destroy Ubel then have all of them dead.

"Not much of a talker are we boys, I could send you out of this trap if you help me, I could reunite you with your family." For a few moments the thought of taking the easy way out was very tempting but he then thought to himself.

No, I can't let the others down! We were chosen together for a reason!

Ubel didn't like how stubborn kids in the 21st century were, with Andrew saying nothing. He focuses on tempting the other three to come and save him but he is giving them one condition.

In the park at Woodsedge the other three were looking around for any type of clue as to where Andrew was taken, as they were beginning to give up looking in the park Sophie realised something.

"Wait why did we run from the Academy in the first place?" The other two looked at each other, why did they not think of this before?

Last to survive

"That's where Ubel is hiding out!"

"Exactly he is bound to be keeping Andrew somewhere in the Academy." As they come to the conclusion they need to get into the Academy, a familiar voice starts ringing though.

"LISTEN WELL CHILDREN AS YOU HAVE ALREADY FOUND OUT I HAVE THE YOUNGEST OF YOU ALREADY, IF YOU WANT TO SEE HIM AGAIN WITH NO HARM COMING TO HIM THEN BE AT THE ACADEMY BEFORE THE NIGHT IS OUT WITH YOUR CHARMS."

All three of the teens look at each other, in the front of their minds they would not waste a minute before taking the charms to the Academy but they knew deep down that doing this would spell the end of their world.

"What do we do, we need to save Andrew but we can't just hand over the charms." said Sophie, the thought and then Jake came up with something.

"I've got an idea but we need to go back to the camp before I tell you, you never know where his Loggerheads are." Justin, Jake and Sophie made their way back to the camp making sure they are not followed, once they are in the camp Sophie makes the trees completely cover the camps area making it practically impossible for anyone else to get in.

"So, what is this idea?" Justin and Sophie watched as Jake pulled out four ordinary stones from his pocket, they looked at him confused.

"I had a feeling that Ubel would try and use one of us to get the other three to handover the charms but what if we gave him fakes."

"Wouldn't he know that they are fakes? He properly knows more about them than we do." Jake then thought about Justin's point then Sophie pops up with an idea.

"Let's call Mr Legna, he says he is to be called when needed, I think this might be a good time." They all agreed and together closed their eyes and spoke the words Sophie read a few hours ago.

"Call on the charm protector, we are in need, to know some of the legends' deeds!" With seconds Mr Legna appeared in front of them.

"What's wrong? Did you find Andrew?"

"No Ubel found him before we did and he is holding Andrew at the Academy until we go with

Last to survive

the charms to hand them over in return for Andrew."

"Ah I see the problem then."

"But Jake had an idea that we could give him fake ones but wouldn't he know if they were fake? After all he has been waiting 100 years for them and we have had them what 2 weeks now"

"That is true Justin however Ubel has never seen the charms so in fact giving over fakes may just work and give you enough time to get Andrew out of there before he realises."

"So, it could work?" Sophie asked hopefully. They all wanted Andrew back safely and unharmed so if it gave them enough time to get him out then they may just take that chance.

"It can work but you need to make it convincing now listen up all of you." The teens listen as their history teacher tells them how to fool the evil sorcerer.

In the Academies sports hall Andrew was still bound and he had been left on his own in the huge dark room, just being left in a dark room was playing on his mind. Andrew has lost all concept of time, he didn't even know how long he had been there, every so often he swore he could see a shadow flying around the room. Andrew jumped as he heard a door a footstep in that slowly get louder, it was only one set so it couldn't be the others already could it? A gentle but spine-chilling laugh echoed through the large room as again the shadow Andrew had been seeing, starts flying around him again.

"I see you have met my friend here boy, by the time your little friends get here you two will be quite acquainted." As Ubel laughs the shadow figure gets closer to Andrew who is struggling to try and get free from the chair he is bound to, he didn't want to get acquainted with anything to do with Ubel because whatever it was spells trouble for him and the others.

Last to survive

Chapter eight

Just outside of the Academy the other three were making their way across the playground, Jake turns to the other two,

"Are you two ready for this?" Both Justin and Sophie nodded.

"Let's hope it works, and remember as soon as we have Andrew one of us goes and gets him out straight away." The boys agree with Sophie, one person has to stick with Andrew like glue in order to get him out safely, they make their way to the front entrance of the Academy.

They walked up the steps towards the sports hall, they could hear the Loggerheads and gathered as much that Andrew was being held in there. As they reached the doors, they looked through the window and as they thought and feared Andrew was in there and the Loggerheads were tormenting him and they also saw Ubel sitting up high on a throne like chair.

"Someone got a big head." The other two could help but giggle at the comment that Justin had just made, Jake then pushed his hand forwards and the doors swung open and Sophie had made some vines whack the Loggerheads away from Andrew. As the Loggerheads tried to attack the teens Justin knocked them over with a blast of water. Ubel stood in front of his throne,

"So, you are here, I must say I was beginning to lose hope."

"Don't underestimate us Ubel!" Ubel laughed at Sophie's statement.

"Well I don't believe I need to, clearly you will give anything to save your own, Now give me the charms!"

"Not even a please, or do evil sorcerers not have any manners."

"Correct, give me the charms!"

"Give us Andrew! Only when he is safe will we give the charms over."

"How do I know you won't just run off with your friend."

"You're the bad guy here, not us, if you want the charms you have no choice." Ubel looks at the teens and for once in his life Ubel agrees and he signals the Loggerhead to release Andrew, Andrew runs over to the others and Jake runs out of the room with him leaving Justin and Sophie behind to catch up.

"Right now, your friend is safe, hand over the charms!" Sophie revealed a small black bag and one by one threw the charms forwards towards Ubel. Once Ubel and his Loggerheads were distracted they quickly slipped out of the sports hall and rushed out of the Academy, they ran across the playground and towards the edge of the forest where Jake and Andrew were waiting.

"Did it work?" asked Jake.

"Like a charm." said Justin, smiling as the four teens ran back through the forest, Andrew was running with them but then got pulled in a different direction by the others.

"We have moved camp, come on!" Andrew then followed the other three to the new camp which he was surprised to see was Justin's house. They all went in and the other three sat down smiling with relief while Andrew just stood there confused.

"Hold on why are you three so relaxed? You just gave over the Charms to Ubel!" They chuckled at Andrew's innocence of the plan they had just carried out; his girlfriend Sophie broke the good news.

"No, we didn't babe, we gave him fakes." Andrews eyes widened.

"Fakes? Surely Ubel will know!" They all smiled, it was Justin's turn to explain.

" It was Jake's idea and we called on Mr Legna or as we have found out Angel, that Ubel has never actually seen the charms so we put a little bit of energy from the real charms into four ordinary rocks to make them look like the colours that the elements are represented by, so by the time he notices we will of been well away."

"But I'm not 13 for another two weeks."

"The even more genius thing cuz, once we entered this house, a protection charm surrounded the house till the moment you turn 13 all we have to do is wait it out."

"But Ubel will see us in here."

"No, he won't babe the protection charm has made this house look like it's just rubble so it's the perfect disguise so not only will we have time to prepare to fight Ubel we also get to make him run around like an idiot, to be honest it will suit him." They all laugh at Sophie's last comment and Andrew starts to relax. The teens settle down to spend the next two weeks learning all they can

Last to survive

about the different kinds of magic they can summon using their charms, they also learn about Ubel and his Loggerheads and the legend they come from.

Back at the Academy Ubel is enjoying his victory and he had the four charms on his pedestal, waiting for the charms to reveal their powers. But two weeks went by and with each day Ubel was getting more and more impatient with the charms, his army of Loggerheads and himself have done nothing but watch what they thought were the charms. It was late at night on the 14th night of waiting when the charms started glowing, Ubel jumped up from his chair;

"THIS IS IT LOGGERHEADS THIS IS THE MOMENT WHERE I UBEL CAN CONTROL ALL OF THE ELEMENTS!" There was a cheer from the Loggerheads for their master, the stones keep glowing brighter and brighter as the Loggerheads chanted for Ubel.

Ubel made his way through his army nearer to the charms, as he got to the pedestal the charms stopped glowing, Ubel signalled for light and when he could then see he saw four ordinary river stones. He started to fill with rage, the anger grew inside of him. How could they have been

Last to survive

tricked by children? His scream of rage sent his Loggerheads running and the teens who now have come out the house heard the scream and just smiled at each other.

"I think Ubel has found out they are fakes." said Sophie smiling

"Well just in time." Andrew said from behind them holding a controlled fireball, the others smiled with relief.

"You can access and control your charm powers."

"Looks like it, now why don't we see what else we can do before Ubel declares war on us." The teens laughed and went off into the community to train their powers even more, giving Andrew time to practice his newly found control.

Back at the Academy Ubel was standing on the roof of the Academy and he summoned a Loggerhead.

"Find them and don't stop until you have all of those brats in your clutches... if they want to play games then fine!" As he watched his army go to hunt the teens down, he smiled,

Last to survive

"We all have a star player children, and mine is closer to you then you think." He looked at the four teens in his staff and focused on Andrew.

Chapter nine

Even though they were thankful that they haven't had much trouble they were wondering what Ubel was up to. They had spent the last few days dodging the Loggerheads that were hunting them down, not to say that they didn't have fun while doing this after they were still young. They were hiding inside the community centre after being followed by four Loggerheads, as the brainless followers of Ubel were looking around confused because they swear, they had seen the four teens. The four teens decide that the Loggerheads need a bit of a cool down so Justin gathers his hands, as he does this the sky fills with rain cloud and they poured rain water down on the Loggerheads,

"Here Sophie, I think that mud down there should join the fun." Sophie smiled and with a wave of her hand the mud nearby expanded and the Loggerheads started slipping and tripping over each other. The teens were laughing so much they nearly forgot to stay out of sight. Little did the teens know Ubel had a secret weapon and in a few hours that weapon would activate.

Last to survive

Later on, in the evening the teen were sat on the steps outside the community centre,

"So, when you do think Ubel will make a move, or do you think he is waiting for us to go back to the school?" Sophie asked.

"I reckon we need to take out the Loggerheads without them, he has no protection." Jake suggested

"That would a good idea if we knew how many there were, he's a sorcerer he properly makes them appear out of nowhere." said Justin. While the other three were discussing what to do next Andrew was very quiet all of a sudden and then randomly spoke,

"I just need to get something to eat." Sophie turned round

"Okay be careful though babe that fake charm trick won't work twice." Andrew walked over to their bag with their food supply and disappeared round the corner.

"Is Andrew okay?" Aske Jake.

"He was snatched 2 weeks ago then had to hide out in my house for two weeks until his powers were under control, he's bound to feel a little off at the moment." Jake could understand what

Last to survive

Justin was saying, it's a lot to go through when you're as young as Andrew. Suddenly they heard a familiar voice that sent a chill down their spine.

"GAME ON CHILDREN."

The three teens looked at each other confused, what was Ubel up to? Andrew came back round slowly and the other turned to see him.

"Hey that was quick cuz." As Justin said this Andrew looked at the other but his eyes were red and this shook the other three as they stepped back.

"Why do I have a feeling Ubel is behind this?" Sophie asked, Andrew then attacked his own friends. The other tried to defend themselves without hurting Andrew too much but they were quickly realising that Andrew was trying to hurt them, Sophie summoned up vines to twist round and trap Andrew by his wrists. Once he was under control, they took a minute to catch their breath.

"Andrew what the hell! You could have hurt us!" Jake shouted, rubbing the back of his head. Justin

Last to survive

and Sophie had no words at this point, not only because they were trying to get their breath back but they were also shocked about what just happened. Why the hell would Andrew try to hurt them? Andrew then looked up with his red eyes and an evil smile on his face.

"Oh, I'm not Andrew." The other three teens looked confused,

"Okay if you're not Andrew then who are you?" asked Justin, Andrew just smiled again before he answered,

"I am your worst nightmare, I am Shadow." The other felt a chill go through them, Who the hell was Shadow.

"So where exactly is Andrew then Shadow?" Sophie asked, Andrew laughed at the question.

"He is still here, let's just say I take advantage of his dark side."

"Andrew doesn't have a dark bone in his body! "exclaimed Justin, he knew his own cousin and Andrew wasn't one to be mean or nasty, he was always loyal to his friends and Sophie and caring to others around him.

"Oh, he does, you all do and soon you will find that out." After this remark Andrew collapsed onto his knees, after a few moments he looked up again with the red eyes gone.

"What...happened..." The others breathed a sigh of relief and Sophie released the vines holding Andrew before throwing her arms around her confused boyfriend. The older two didn't really know how to explain what had just happened.

"You were well... possessed by something mate." Andrew looked at Jake and Justin

"What?"

"It's true cuz you were not yourself you came back round from the corner with red eyes and an evil smile on your face and tried to attack us, but thankfully Sophie was quick to tie you down controlling whatever was in you with her vine's." Andrew looked at his wrists that were red from where he had vine round them a few minutes before, Sophie looked guilty

"Sorry, you were about to hurt us and I knew you wouldn't be able to live with yourself." Andrew put an arm around Sophie.

"It's okay by the sounds of it, you did the right thing, I don't think I could have forgiven myself if I had hurt you." They looked at each other and for

Last to survive

the first time in their time dating Sophie and Andrew kissed each other, for a moment they forgot about what was happening around them. The kiss only lasted a few short moments but to them it felt like a lifetime, for both of them it was their first kiss so it was special. Justin and Jake watched on, Justin could only think of one thing to say,

"Young love eh Jake." Jake just nodded smiling. The four teens decided to go back to the house and make a plan to face Ubel once and destroy him once and for all so they can go back to their normal lives. They had started to realise how much they took for granted in their everyday lives even the smaller things, like their parents say morning and goodnight to them each day, walking to school and having their classes. Even Justin and Jake were missing going to school each day, having lunch with their friends and being able to go home and be normal teenagers. Instead they were on their own in Woodsedge with the fate of the whole community, the whole world in their hands. They didn't want the responsibility of the whole world on their shoulders but they grew to accept that they didn't have much of a choice, all four of them believed that everyone had a purpose in life but they didn't realise this would be theirs.

Chapter ten

It had been a few days since Shadow appeared in Andrew, the teens were very careful and decided it would be best if Andrew did not leave their sight until they could figure out how to get rid of Shadow from his body. Sophie had been reading up on the legend again just in case they had missed anything but she didn't find any clue to who Shadow was, she then thought about going to see if she can find out who Shadow is by spying at the Academy.

"You want to willingly go back to the Academy." exclaimed Justin after Sophie suggested her idea to the boys.

"Well how else are we going to find out about Shadow and how to get rid of it from Andrew? There is nothing in the legends book about it."

"Why don't we ask Mr Legna?" suggested Jake.

"I already tried but he didn't come when I called." Sophie said with her head lowered, the boy's eyes widened because now not only did they have some sort of demon in one of them but now the sacred protector of the charms is not responding.

Last to survive

"So, we're on our own?" asked Andrew, worried at this point because it was better when they knew they could call on their history teacher but now they are completely on their own he was more frightened like when they first discovered where they were.

"I suppose Sophie is right then if we are on our own, we don't have much of a choice we have to go to the academy." said Jake.

"But we need a plan," said Sophie. The four teens sat down and started to discuss going to the academy and finding out more about Shadow, the demon currently in Andrew. Little do they know that Ubel had a plan of his own to get back at the teens and this time he was settling for anything but the real charms and if that meant getting rid of the four teens once and for all.

In the next few days, the four teens decided to get some training in with their charms before going to face Ubel and his army of Loggerheads. They headed down to the forest and found a clearing to practice in, they spent the next few hours practicing to harness their charms. They hoped with enough time practicing together they can mould their powers as one, this is something they remember being told can happen if they work together. As they were training Shadow began to try and take control of Andrews mind and body again but this time Shadow was clever and did not make himself known.

Shadow was looking through Andrew's eyes when he saw that Andrew kept looking at Sophie. He then thought of a plan to get Ubel's target to the Academy, instead of putting an evil thought in Andrew's brain he does the opposite by making Andrew think of taking Sophie on a walk later that evening. When they go back to the house the teens are having some food and drink when Andrew came over and sat next to his girlfriend,

"Hey do you fancy going for a walk later on just me and you?" Sophie looked at her boyfriend and smiled, she had to admit it would be nice to spend even a little time with Andrew on their own.

"Yeah sure okay." Andrew smiled and let Sophie carry on reading the Legends book. Sophie carried on reading the page she was on, it told her of a child that was a descendant from the mother of the Four original sorcerers, this child could harness all of the powers form all elements not just one. This child will be the most powerful

Last to survive

sorcerer since the original Four Sorcerers. Sophie smiled, maybe one day they will meet this child.

Later on, that night Andrew and Sophie went out into the community, they decided to get some more food from the shop on their way back from their walk. They did stop at a shop to get some treats for their walk, as they were walking, they went past Sophie's house, she stopped. Andrew turned to see her looking up at her house. He went back over to Sophie who for the first time since they ended up in this battle thought mainly about how much she missed her mum and stepdad, a few tears trickled down her cheeks as she thought about her parents.

"Hey you will see them again."

"I know but we don't know, when do we?" Andrew didn't have an answer because frankly Sophie was right, they didn't know when they were going to see their families again, the fight was far from over and at this moment in time they didn't see the end of it arriving anytime soon. They carried on walking and went up to the community centre, once there they sat on the big steps that surround the community centre. For about an hour they forgot all about everything going on around them. Shadow was lurking within

Last to survive

Andrews body waiting for his time to strike, Sophie turned to pick up her bag,

"I think we had better get back Justin and Jake will be wondering where we are." Shadow had risen from the depths of Andrews body and without Sophie realising he had completely taken over Andrews mind and body. He reached for Sophie's hand and took hold of it, as she turned round to look at her boyfriend a chill went down her when she saw his eyes were red.

"Shadow!"

Andrew smiled evilly as Sophie tried to pull away.

"Hello Sophie, miss me?" Sophie managed to pull away from Andrew, she then got a charm and set off a burst of energy in the sky, they had read in the Legends book about how they can send signals to each other if they were on their own and were attacked. Over at the house Justin and Jake saw the green flash in the sky,

"Sophie and Andrew are being attacked!" Justin watched the sky and he didn't see any red bursts in the sky.

"No Jake I think a certain trouble maker is back." They made their way to the community centre as fast as they could.

Last to survive

Sophie on the other hand was facing Shadow on her own, she didn't want to hurt Andrew but it didn't look as if she a choice, Andrew lunged for Sophie but she jumped down from the steps as she turned around Andrew had a fireball in his hand but Sophie stamped one of feet on the ground causing Andrew to fall down off of his feet. While he was on the ground Sophie took her chance to run, she didn't want to hurt Andrew so she had to avoid him until the other two got there. As she reached the basketball court she could feel Andrew following her but she couldn't risk turning round to see if Shadow had gone, as she going across the basketball court Sophie is stopped by a wall of fire forcing her to turn around and come face to face with a possessed Andrew who's eyes were glowing red, with an evil look on his face he slowly walked towards Sophie. As Justin and Jake reached the fire Justin put it out with a water blast from his charm, as they got through into the basketball court Andrew and Sophie disappeared in front of eyes, they saw both the looks and red eyes on Andrew and the terrified look on Sophie's face. They were gutted they didn't make it in time but they knew where Sophie would have been taken, both boys make their way to the Academy.

Chapter eleven

At the Academy Sophie woke up to find herself in an empty room, one that she didn't recognise as she got up, she looked around but couldn't see very much.

"I guess Ubel has made a few changes to the Academy." Sophie said to herself. The room then lit up with old fashioned touches on the walls one by one surrounding her.

"I know you're there Ubel, show yourself!" shouted Sophie, a laugh echoed through the room.

"Smart girl but no I do not give in to demands from children, if you want to see me Sophie you come and find me...if you can." After hearing Ubel's message Sophie was left confused, she was in a locked room how could she find him? She tried to open the door but had no luck, as she was facing the door, she heard the gushing of water as she looked round, she could see water pouring in, horror shot over her face as the water came towards her. Sophie started to panic as the water got deeper and deeper, when it was at her knees her charm started glowing and a shot of energy burst out and lit up the top of the room. The

Last to survive

room didn't even have a ceiling. If she could find a way to stay on top of the water's surface she could jump over the wall, but how? Getting her charm out of her pocket she thought as the water level rose quickly, then while holding the stone she tried something.

Stop this strife

Help me save my life

Out of wood and vines

Build me a boat

So out of here safely I will float!

After a few moments Sophie watched as a boat magically started forming in front of her, quickly she got into the boat before water completely covered her over. As the water level rose so did, she in the boat, before long she was at the top and as the water fell over the walls, she was pulled over the top in the boat. As the boat was about to fall, she got up and jumped, Sophie rolled as she landed in the one of the corridors of the Academy. Sophie got up and ran towards the exit, she got to the middle part of the Academy

Last to survive

where the principal's office was placed as she tried to leave though one of the doors, they all slammed shut trapping her again.

Sophie looked round for a way out but to her horror large vines covered in thorns started to cover the exits and they also started making their way into the room. Sophie was shocked because she thought that she controlled the earth element. She tried to stop the vines but couldn't. That's when she heard that familiar evil laugh.

"So, I couldn't drown you, maybe your own element will end you once and for all!" As Ubel's evil laugh fades away Sophie looks around and watches as the thorn covered vines start to cover the room getting closer to her.

"How the hell am I going to fight off my own element." The vines were starting to attack Sophie; she managed to break off some of the stairway banister to keep the vines at bay. She could feel something burning inside of her but she didn't know what until she throws her hands forward accidentally and a fireball came out of her hands. She looked shocked as it slowly burned away some of the vines, Sophie knew she didn't have time to think why she could control fire so she kept sending fireballs into the vines,

Last to survive

eventually she could get to one of the doors. The door was still locked shut; Sophie kept trying to get it open but she wasn't having any luck.

Sophie stepped back from the door and she thought about her new found abilities,

"Does this mean I can control all of the elements, am I the child that I read about." Sophie though for a second, she had to think of a way to get the door open, she looked at the door and focused.

Help me escape the vine tree

Use the power of wind

To open the door

And set me free!

A gust of wind flew past Sophie and blew the doors wide open; Sophie ran through down the corridor. She reached the Academy's dining hall where she was met again with a possessed Andrew. Andrews eyes were glowing red, Sophie had a feeling she knew what element she would be facing next. The same familiar spine-chilling evil laugh echoed through the hall; Sophie turned to see Ubel.

Last to survive

"Andrew is too strong to let Shadow hurt me!" Sophie shouted, Ubel laughed and her outburst.

"Oh, I know, I wasn't going to take that chance no no no this is purely an illusion but the fire it produces is very real, I hope you like the heat Sophie!" Ubel disappeared leaving Sophie in the hall where slowly the walls slowly started to burn spreading onto the floor.

"Yeah I like heat Ubel but this takes the biscuit." Sophie says to herself as she watches the flames grow and expand nearer to her. She closed her eyes,

My life again I must save

Stop this fire

With an ocean wave!

Just as the fire was brushing Sophie's leg she screamed, after a few moments a wave of water swept across the hall extinguishing the fire as it flowed across the hall, when Sophie opened her eyes and saw the room was knee high in ocean water. As Sophie waded herself through, she could smell the sea salt in the room. She forced the door open and ran out the door and as the water flowed out into the playground. Sophie saw across the playground Andrew walking out of the Academy but he looked as if he was in a trance, she went to run across the playground but then found herself surrounded by Loggerheads.

"Oh, not these idiots again." Sophie got out her charm and made the sky flash green, she knew that the boys would see it.

"Well at least they know I'm still alive." Sophie then turned her attention to fighting the Loggerhead, praying in her head that the boys wouldn't be very long.

Back by the park next to the Academy Justin and Jake ran round the corner and saw someone on the ground by the park entrance.

"Isn't that Andrew?" The boy ran over to Andrew just as he was waking up, he looked at Justin and Jake then went from confused to worried.

"Don't say it...please." The older two didn't want too but Andrew needed to know.

"Shadow took over your body this time but you took Sophie to the Academy." Andrews eyes widened.

Last to survive

"She's not…."

"No, she's still alive she just sent a green flash in the sky, we don't have time we need to get to Sophie and get her out of the Academy." With Justin's words in his head Andrew got up on his feet and along with Justin and Jake ran to the Academy.

Last to survive

Chapter twelve

As the boys ran to the Academy the sky over Woodsedge was filled with dark thunder clouds, it was as if Woodsedge itself was coming to life and knew a battle was coming. Each of the teens also knew that their first big fight was starting, clearly Ubel is tired of playing games and so were they. At the entrance to the Academy grounds Andrew stopped Justin and Jake turned around and saw him just stood staring at the Academy, he looked up at the place he used to feel safe but now his body couldn't even step into its grounds, he was paralysed with fear and guilt that he was the reason Sophie was in there. As they all faced the Academy, they could see Sophie in the distance on the playground trying her best to fight off the Loggerheads but she was struggling. Justin turned to Andrew,

"We need to get in there Sophie is struggling!" Andrew was still frozen to the ground.

"I…. I can't it's my fault that Sophie is in there!" Justin looked at his petrified cousin, he needed to get him in there.

"Listen Andrew your girlfriend is up there right now fighting on her own and we don't get in

Last to survive

there she will be dead because the Loggerheads will kill her!" Andrew realised that Justin was right and the last thing he wanted was to leave here without Sophie, he watched on for a few moments as she tried to fight off the Loggerheads but she was thrown to the floor, the boys had seen enough and they all ran in after Sophie.

On the playground as Sophie turned her head, she was relieved to see the boys coming up the pathway, she then felt a hand grab her and pull her up and keep hold of her. She was too tired to fight back and by this time she was praying that the boys could save her. The boys reached the playground and their worst fears were confirmed, Ubel had a hold of Sophie who looked physically and mentally too tired to carry on fighting with his Loggerheads between him and the boy's. Guilt flooded Andrew as he watched Sophie struggle to even stand up,

"Let Sophie go!" Andrew shouted. Ubel laughed, the Loggerheads surrounded the boys.

"Do you think I am going to fall for any sly trick again oh no you will answer to me now, I will release the girl once I have the REAL charms!" The boys looked at each other, Ubel had them cornered. Mr Legna was nowhere to be seen,

Last to survive

Sophie was on the brink of collapse because she was so exhausted from all the fighting and could not even fight off Ubel's grasp on her. It didn't look as if they had any choice but to give in, they pray that if they do Ubel may just show some mercy and let them have their normal lives back. Andrew stepped forward.

"If we give you the charms, the real one you let Sophie go and you give us time to let her recover before you use them." Ubel Smiled, he was winning. The teens were going to give over the charms to save Sophie's life which looked as if it was drowning by the minute. Each of them took out their charms, Sophie looked on and like the boys she thought this was it, Ubel had won.

Ubel already had Sophie's charm, one by one the boys threw the charms towards Ubel who then let Sophie drop to the ground. The boys took their chance to run over to Sophie, they watched as Ubel picked up the other three charms.

"Those are the real charms Ubel, you have our word now let us go." Justin said, helping get Sophie on her feet. Ubel turned to the teens,

"Very well you may leave the Academy with the girl but I would make the most of the time you four kids have left because next time you won't be so lucky." With that said Ubel and his loggerhead army disappeared with a strike of thunder and lightning.

"Come on we need to get out of here." said Jake. The boys helped Sophie back to Justin's house, they practically carried Sophie back because she was too weak to hold her own weight. As they got back Andrew watched as Justin and Jake put Sophie on the big sofa as one of them brushed her leg she screamed.

"What wrong?" Jake asked Sophie.

"My... leg...its...burnt." Sophie said weakly between her breaths. The boys looked at her leg, Sophie happened to have a dress on so no fabric was burnt into her skin but they did see a massive blistering red burn up the bottom of her leg. The Boys didn't know what to do, Sophie was usually the one they knew first aid, Andrew then took a breath then stepped forward.

"You need to go to the chemist, get as much first aid stuff you can carry, especially stuff for burns, as painkillers too just everything you can!" Justin and Jake didn't argue and they left the house and made their way to the local Chemist. Thankfully the one thing that made them still think this was Woodsedge is that all of the shops and businesses

Last to survive

still had everything in them. Andrew knelt down next to Sophie, tears in his eyes. He felt so guilty, if he hadn't stormed off weeks ago then Ubel wouldn't have been able to put Shadow inside him therefore Ubel wouldn't have got his hands-on Sophie so easily.

Sophie had fallen asleep while they waited for Jake and Justin to get back with the first aid supplies. Andrew was sat by Sophie watching and waiting,

"I'm sorry Sophie, I never meant for any of this to happen. You know you getting hurt if anything I wanted to protect you, when we get out of this mess, I will be the best boyfriend you have had. I know I can have a bit of a temper but I would never hurt you, your so kind and open minded…sometimes I think your too good for me, how did a silly boy like me end up with a girl like you eh…. I don't even know why I'm saying this now while you're sleeping but I really do think the world of you… I love you Sophie…" Andrew lowered his head, after a few moments he heard a small weak voice.

"I love you too." Andrew looked up to see Sophie was awake but still weak but she was smiling.

Last to survive

"You heard all of that then?" Sophie nodded.

"Yeah I heard it... you aint half soppy at times." Andrew laughed lightly, Sophie then reached out and took one of Andrew's hands.

"I'm sorry you got hurt." Sophie looked Andrew in his eyes, she could see that he was riddled with guilt.

"It's not your fault Andrew, I think we all knew that we weren't going to come out of this unscared were we." Andrew knew Sophie was right but he couldn't help but let the tears fall from his eyes and down his cheeks.

"Hey don't cry you will set me off... now make yourself useful and fetch me some water." Andrew laughed lightly and got up to get Sophie some water from the kitchen, he had to admire how Sophie can still be so strong after everything that has happened.

After about an hour Justin and Jake got back with a load of supplies, they emptied out the stuff they got on the floor of the front room.

"We figured we would get some food as well while we were there, we basically grabbed what we could carry but we did get a few of everything

Last to survive

to do with first aid in the chemists as well and there were some leaflets on how to treat different things like burns and that." The boys searched for everything they needed, they gave Sophie some painkillers and started treating her burn on her leg. Sophie had a little more energy now so when the boys were stuck, she could help them out. Later on, that evening Sophie's leg was all bandaged up, she still couldn't put any weight on it without getting any pain but at the moment the teens were cautious to leave the house at the moment. Now Ubel had the charms they believed that it was the end.

One question was going through each of their minds though and finally Andrew said what they were all thinking.

"Where was Mr Legna then when we needed him?" The other three did not have an answer, only the same question. After all Mr Lagna did say that he would appear if they called him when they needed him the most. So why did he not help them this time? Was something or someone stopping him?

"Maybe he was one of Ubel's tricks this whole time." said Justin.

Last to survive

"No, he couldn't be remember, because I charmed the vines to attack anyone evil or bad and he could get through." said Sophie.

"Then like Andrew said, where is he?" Then teens couldn't only hope that he would turn up again, he had to because he was the protector of the Charms. He will know if they have fallen into the wrong hands. What they didn't realise was Mr Legna was helping from within,

"You were right, they gave up the Charms to save the girl." Ubel exclaimed, as he turned around Ubel looked at Mr Legna who smiled back.

"Of course, Master they will do anything to save the girl, it's a protective nature they have."

"I should strike them now while they are weak." Mr Legna shook his head.

"No master if I were you, I would relax, wait a while after all you now possess the charms, if anything they will get more and more paranoid the longer you make them wait then they will give up and think you have left them alone, then you strike."

Last to survive

Chapter thirteen

Later on, that night Justin, Andrew and Sophie were asleep, Jake was still awake listening out for any sign of Ubel or his Loggerheads. After a while Jake nodded off and he found himself engulfed in a dream, but this dream was different. It almost seemed real, he was back at the Academy, the floor was covered in smoke and there was one light coming from the back of the lunch hall. Jake's mind told him to wake up or walk the other way but he found himself walking towards the lunch hall, looking in through the window he saw Ubel and Mr Legna together talking.

Jake moved up by the door and listened into the conversation,

"Now you have the charms master the children are vulnerable, they will be powerless."

"Exactly and now with you on my side they have nothing to help them."

"I am indeed master, it's like they are now more toys for you to play with and torment until you are bored." Jakes eyes widened with shock,

Last to survive

"Please say that Justin wasn't right please let this just be a dream." Jake whispered to himself. As he listened to the conversation, they were making a plan to strike the teens when they were least expecting it, while they were talking a loggerhead came up to them. After a few moments they all turned to look straight at Jake.

"Uh oh." Jake got up and started running out of the academy, he was then stopped in his path by three bodies. When the smoke cleared away it was Justin, Sophie and Andrew on the ground... they were not moving.

"GET HIM!" Jake jumped over the bodies of his friends and turned round as he tripped a fell to the floor.

Jake then woke up with a jump, he was sweating and tried to get his breath back. As he looked round, he saw that Andrew and Sophie were still asleep, but there was no sign of Justin, Jake got up and went into the kitchen and breathed a sigh of relief to find Justin standing there with a drink.

"Couldn't sleep?" Justin nodded while taking a sip from his drink.

Last to survive

"Yeah then I saw you had nodded off so I stayed awake, you okay you look a little flushed mate." Jake nodded,

"Yeah but I hope it was just a dream though."

"Why what happened?" Jake got himself some water before he told Justin what happened.

"I was at the Academy and I saw Ubel with Mr Legna but they were working together but the dream seemed real, we have to check it out." Justin sighed, was he, really right? Had Mr Legna been playing them this whole time? Either way at this moment in time the one person that as right was Jake, they did need to see if this is true. But it did mean they would have to go back to the Academy…. Without no charms or powers to fight Ubel and his Loggerheads. Then they heard a voice at the door,

"What's going on?" The boys turned round to see Sophie and Andrew stood in the doorway.

"Sophie you're on your feet again I thought it was too painful to walk on." said Jake.

"Exactly it was too painful but I've been on that sofa for two days, now are you two gunna answer my question." Justin and Jake looked at each other, Jake then began to tell Sophie and Andrew

Last to survive

about his dream that he had and how real it felt. Sophie and Andrew agreed that they need to find out once and for all whose side Mr Legna is really on.

They decide to wait till morning and head to the Academy during the day as they have noticed a lot of the altercations, they have with Ubel happen at night so they assume that his body clock and his army must sleep during the day. This is what they were hoping at least. The next morning, they start their journey to the Academy and they decide to cut through the forest instead of out in the open in the community. As they were walking up the hill, they saw a man that they hadn't seen before, they all got down low and snuck up to the top of the path, Sophie's eyes widened when the man performed magic and turned so, they saw his face... It was her stepdad.

"Mark!" Mark turned round to see his stepdaughter standing with her friends. Sophie ran up to her stepfather and they both wrapped their arms around each other, when they broke off their hug Mark looked at the Teens.

"Where is Ubel then?" They all looked at Mark confused; how did he know about Ubel?

Last to survive

"Uhhhhh."

"Come on, we have no time to waste, we need to get those charms back." As Mark turned round to see the Teens still looking confused, Mark sighed and realised that some details have been missed out.

"I'm already guessing that you know a family was charged over 100 years ago to look over the element charms to protect them from danger, by the original four sorcerers. Well while the last Sorcerer before they died, who controlled the earth element saw that the family were trying to use it for their selfish needs, they had believed Ubel about making the charms reach their potential in other words using them for power instead of protection. Well this sorcerer ended up trusting another close friend from the next village across the forest to watch over from the side lines, another sorcerer, my ancestors and the night that Ubel invaded the village it wasn't Mr Legna that put the charms into hiding, it was my ancestor. Mr Legna turned to the dark side years ago, but he was very convincing. He posed as the good guy this whole time waiting for his master, while my family has been serving as a human prison for Ubel but as you can see, he got out and we have to stop them."

"But Mark Ubel has charms, at the academy. We don't have any power anymore." Mark smiled.

"You do have power, not only do you still have the power of elements but you have a stronger power, one the Ubel could only ever wish to have." Again, the Teens look confused.

"But the charms."

"And what other power would we have?" Mark smiled.

"Do you four realise why the charms choose you?" They all thought about it, they couldn't really think what it could be, Mark chuckled.

"Look the original four sorcerers were not family not by blood anyway, they were close friends. It was friendship that made them more powerful. That's why the charms choose you, plus the charms when they found you would have dispersed the powers into you."

"So, we have had the powers this whole time?" asked Andrew

"Yes."

"Then if you were the real protector why didn't you come to us when we needed you when I was

Last to survive

being held up and nearly burnt alive?" Sophie asked her stepfather.

"Well be fair Sophie when someone breaks out of your body it tends to leave you unconscious for a while, I only just woke up a few hours ago. Now come along all of you, we have work to do if we are to send Ubel back from where he came from."

Mark started walking and the teens followed on.

Meanwhile in the Academy Ubel and Mr Legna were watching them come towards the Academy.

"Mr Legna, prepare the Loggerheads we have a battle to look forward to."

"Yes master, right away." Mr Legna left the room and started walking down the corridor,

"And what final battle it will be."

Chapter fourteen

As they were walking to the Academy the teens started having doubts in their minds. Can they trust Mark? They thought that they could trust Mr Legna but it turns out he was on Ubel's' side. No had told them the whole story just yet, not even Mark had told them everything. Sophie took on herself to just come out with what they were all thinking, after all he was her stepfather, she felt obliged to ask.

"Mark what is the full story? Completely." Mark stopped and turned round to the teens.

"I told you the story Sophie, now come on we don't have time for this."

"No, we need to know that we can trust you, surely you can't blame us after thinking we could trust Mr Legna. We still have questions and I have an important one as well, we won't go anywhere until we know we can trust you." Mark sighed and smiled to himself, Sophie was so much like her mother it was scary sometimes. Like Sophie, her mum may give off that she is quiet and polite but inside they are both just as fiery, brave and completely loyal to their friends and family, one thing they both do is stick to their words.

Last to survive

"Very well, but not out here." They were close to Sophie's house so went in there so Mark could finally reveal everything about the Woodsedge legend. It took hours for him to tell them in detail about the village that once stood in the forest and the arrival of Ubel, up to the night he and his army invaded and burned the village to the ground.

"You see my ancestors were not killed in the attack because Ubel thought that it was only that village that played a part in protecting the charms, the village was always securely guarded after they discovered what Ubel's intentions were. What they didn't know was that Mr Legna or Angel as he was known then had turned to the dark side himself, he agreed to help get Ubel's army in. It was on one of his trips to visit his dying friend that my ancestors overheard the conversation between Mr Legna and Ubel."

"And is that when your family was also trusted?" Justin asked.

"Yes, a few months after the attack Ubel nearly located the charms so my ancestors took it upon themselves to trap him in their own body, deep inside where he couldn't do any harm, the one spanner in that plan was that the next descendant in the family would have to then receive Ubel and keep him away from the rest of the world, when they came of age of course and as the times grew so did the age to trap Ubel."

"How old were you?" Andrew asked.

"I was 18 years old when it was my turn, trust me it is no easy task either. The first few months I had to keep myself away from society and my loved ones so that I could get Ubel under control inside of me, being a human prison wasn't fun, sometimes it felt like I was burning from the inside, he would mess with my mind the first few weeks trying to convince me to let him out but I stayed strong."

"So how did he get out then?" Jake asked, Mark sighed.

"When you are a human prison as it were, your resistance weakens as you get older so I suppose Ubel took advantage when he had the chance, Mr Legna waiting for his master faithfully when he did escape."

"But you are not even that old though, you're the same age as my mum." Mark had to chuckle at Sophie's statement.

Last to survive

"Well inheriting my family's magic gives me an advantage so I am a lot older than I look, what was this other question you wanted to ask?" The boys looked at Sophie because even they were not aware of this question.

"Is there meant to be a child one day that can wield all of the elements?" Mark sat back in his chair.

"What? Oh, you mean Mother Nature's descendent. Yeah there is a tale that one day in the 21st century a child was to be born that could wield all the elements, said to be more powerful than all four of the elements together." Sophie's eyes widened, "Why do ask?"

"Because I think I might be that child." They all looked at Sophie, the boy's eyes were wide with shock.

"What makes you think that Sophie?" Mark asked. Now it was Sophie's turn to tell and story.

"When Ubel was holding me in the Academy it wasn't just tied down on a chair like Andrew was, I had to fight my way through different rooms that had what I could only describe as evil versions of the elements. The first room I didn't think anything of it but in the second room it was the earth element and that's what I usually have the power for with my charm but I wasn't going to get anywhere this time, I climbed the stairs but tripped as I turned round I put my hands up and fireballs appeared burning up all the vines trying to attack me, I used the air element to get out of the room and then the final room he had Andrew in there with shadow possessing him. The room was set on fire and it spread faster and closer towards me, that's when I used the water element that one was a little delayed so I got burned up my leg but eventually I was able to escape all the rooms only to be meet with the loggerheads and well I can't remember much more by body just collapsed."

"You just strained yourself that's all, it's common when you haven't had powers for very long. But yes, if what you're describing is true then it is highly likely that you are that child, you are Mother Nature's descendant."

It was a lot to take in for everyone, mostly Sophie. Mark explained that Ubel properly already knew that Sophie was mother nature's descent which is why she was trapped in the rooms he was hoping that one of them would destroy her.

Last to survive

"But why would they need Sophie destroyed first?" Andrew asked, taking a hold of Sophie's hand.

"Because it leaves the powers open for anyone to have and all together the elements generate enough powers to be able to take over this world."

"One other thing, where is everyone that was in Woodsedge? Where is mum?" Mark sighed,

"Most likely some empty dimension somewhere in time and space but when you defeat Ubel they will all come back, and they will remember nothing it will be as if it was just after the storm, you four will also wake up where it first started."

"In the park?" Justin asked, Mark nodded. Sophie took a breath,

"So how do we do this then? How do we defeat Ubel and bring everyone back to Woodsedge?"

"You have to face Ubel and his army of Loggerheads head on and then when he is vulnerable and you will know when, use this spell Make sure you surround him. It won't kill him but it will make sure he never disturbs anyone ever again." Mark handed a piece of paper that looked like it was torn from a book, on it was a spell. The teens stood tall but, on the inside, they were scared beyond belief, only one side was coming out of this battle and they were praying it was going to be them.

At the academy Ubel was in the sports hall, Mr Legna entered the room and made his way through the loggerheads.

"We are ready, master every Loggerhead is ready for battle." Ubel smiled while looking into his staff watching the teens make their way to the academy.

"Oh, children you have no idea what you are walking into." Ubel turns to Mr Legna once more,

"And our family will finally have what we deserve after all these years."

"Indeed, we will brother."

Last to survive

Chapter fifteen

The four teens made their way to the Academy. As they walked through Woodsedge, they took it all in properly, every house, every shop and forest area, they then stopped by the very same park they were in before the storm that took everyone but them out of the community.

"So, this is it then." Andrew said as they all looked over the park and could see the top of the Academy. Scared would be an understatement to describe how they were feeling right now, they knew that it was going to be them or Ubel coming out victorious.

"We will win though, we will beat Ubel and get everyone back." Sophie said, her voice was wobbling but she was hoping that what she just said was going to be true.

"Sophie's right I mean we were chosen by the charms like Mark said we have on our side." Everyone knew that Justin was on about their friendship, it had seen them through some battles at school but never a battle like not where they could….

Last to survive

They carried on to the Academy and reached the Ubel's Loggerheads or even Ubel himself. They got to the front playground of the academy and stopped,

"So where do we start?" Jake asked.

"There's no point sneaking in Ubel and his loggerheads could be anywhere." Justin said, they went into the Academy via the lunch hall. It was dark and cold; they could see the burn marks from where the fire was here that nearly killed Sophie. Sophie shivered; last time she was at the academy she was battling to save her life. Now they were back again battling for not just them but everyone in the community, their families, friends, teachers, classmates and neighbours. They reached the steps to the sports hall and as they were half way up they were blown backwards down the steps.

"Well Ubel is in then." said Jake and as they all got back on their feet. They carried on again up the stairs, they started to feel hot, they were looking around but couldn't see any fire.

The teens had made it to the sports hall but it was pitch black,

Last to survive

"Is he even here?" Andrew asked. Suddenly one by one a torch lit up about them all over the sports hall, as they could start to see Ubel's army of loggerheads all around them, they were outnumbered but no one knew how many. Just then they heard the same unfriendly voice that sent a chill down their spine.

"Welcome back! As you can see, I have made a few changes. This building was a little modern for my liking, and now there's just one more thing to make my plan complete. That my dear children is destroying you! Loggerheads get them!" Ubel Shouted, the loggerheads started coming closer towards the teens.

"Okay boys no holding back! We need to get these clowns out of the way."

"Sophie's right the more of his army we defeat the less defence Ubel has." The teens as Sophie said did not hold back, they fought their way through the Loggerheads sometimes needing to use their powers. Ubel watched on with shock with Mr Legna by his side,

"I thought I had the charms now! Why can they still use the powers!" Ubel shouted,

"I do not know brother." answered Mr Legna as he watched in shock horror, how did the teens manage to retain their powers without the charms, how are they still strong. The four teens blasted straight through the last four loggerheads using their element powers, as the last four loggerheads fell to the ground the teens watched as Ubel and Mr Legna made their way towards them.

"Well well well you kids seem to have managed to retain your powers, remarkably truly. How did you manage to still channel the elements when I have the charms!" Ubel demanded.

"The charms hold the powers of the elements unless again you gave us fakes!" Mr Legna added.

"Oh no they were the real charms, but they only held the power till the next four were chosen to wield the elements." said Sophie

"To think we trusted you Mr Legna or should I say Angel…. You see when you were found to be working with Ubel another family was trusted to protect the charms and you lied about hiding the charms." Justin said, Sophie stepped forwards

"My stepfather's family, you see it's passed down you were found out back before Ubel burned the Woodsedge village down."

Last to survive

"The night we found the power transferred from the charms to us." said Andrew

"So, we hold the power so all you have now are some pretty coloured rocks; they don't do anything unless they are in our hands." said Jake.

"We started to suspect you weren't on our side when you didn't appear despite us calling you like you told us to! When Sophie was nearly killed at the hands of Ubel." said Justin.

"And it turns out we were right!" shouted Sophie. Ubel was furious not only at himself but also Mr Legna who had unknowingly got himself caught all those years ago and neither of them had a clue. Mr Legna stepped forwards towards Sophie,

"But we still have a chance brother because this young lady here is the descendant of mother nature herself and if we end the descendant line then the powers are anyone's to claim." Mr Legna went to strike for Sophie but before he could lay a finger on her Jake used his wind power to push him back and pinned up against a wall then Andrew stepped forward.

"You look a little cold there Mr Legna, shame you won't be able to teach this part of history." Andrew for once let his anger take over and threw forward a blast of fire engulfing Mr Legna

Last to survive

in the flames, a few moments later he was nothing but a pile of ash on the floor.

It was just the teens and Ubel left. Ubel looked around him as the teens surrounded him,

"You kids don't honestly think you can beat me!" Ubel shouted with a slight shake in her voice.

"Oh, we like our chances now, you see not only did you get everyone else to do your dirty work but you're also getting on a bit aren't you Ubel?" asked Justin.

"What difference does it make that I'm older, your children, kids. You will never beat a powerful sorcerer!"

"Powerful, by our knowledge the older you get the weaker you become." said Andrew

"That is most likely why you didn't ever do your own dirty work because you didn't have the strength." said Jake.

"We also have another power the binds us together something that only you can ever dream of." said Justin

"And what's that?" asked Ubel

Last to survive

"Friendship." said Andrew. The teens stopped and got into their positions.

"What are you doing?" asked Ubel with a shaky voice.

"We are sending you where you can't hurt anyone else." said Sophie and they all looked at each other and nodded. They then spoke in unison,

This banishment is commanded by the chosen four

To open the time and space door

Take Ubel through to be trapped alone

To pay for his crimes to human kind forevermore

Never to release

So that now the world can now and forever live in peace

A bright white ring surrounded Ubel, as it got closer, they could hear Ubel's screams for help and mercy, the teens had beaten him, as the white ring connected with Ubel the whole sports

Last to survive

hall went white and the teens were thrown back by a blast of energy.

Last to survive

Chapter sixteen

"I think they head to park after school over here!"

"There they are under the climbing frame!"

"Are they okay?!"

"There! lying down quickly someone called the ambulance crew over here to check them out!"

This was what the teens could hear, and the voices were warming and familiar, it was their parents! Which could only mean that the spell worked. Ubel was gone, everyone was back, they had won. They had survived. As they sat up, they were surrounded by their parents, their principal who was the last person to see the teens leave the school and an ambulance crew. They were helped out from under the climbing frame, one by one they were all checked over and the Ambulance told their parents that they were extremely lucky and it was a good idea to hide under the climbing frames as there was massive chunks of debris and sheets of glass all over the park. The teens had only woken up with a few cuts and bruises from small pieces of debris. The principal came up to the teens after they were all checked.

"Well I'm glad that you four are all right and there is better news for you Sophie, it turned out your stepfather had just gone on a trip for a job interview but forgot to tell your mother, he has just this moment come back. I will see you all at school fresh on Monday morning at school. Oh, and you will need to bring in your own lunch for two weeks. Some wiring went during the storm and set the whole lunch hall a blaze." The teens looked at each other and when everyone wasn't listening Jake spoke up

"I don't think it was the wiring that burned the lunch hall." They all went to their homes and were told to rest for the next few days.

The next Monday the teens went back to school, the first thing they all wanted to check was who the new history teacher was. At lunchtime they opened the door to find Mark standing in the classroom.

Last to survive

"Mark! You're the new history teacher?" Sophie asked. Mark smiled and pointed at the door which shut on its own.

"Yes, I am, only seems fitting as like that now pile of ash, I have lived through most of what you learn about or heard about it from my parents." The teens were relieved to see that Mr Legna didn't make a surprised come back,

"Now you four I will warn you for your own safety being the new element sorcerers your powers are only active when they need to be and you need to keep this between yourselves, when you reach 25 years old though you will only remember all of this as a game you played as kids together." The teens understood why, especially after what they had just been through, they were hoping to never need to use their powers again.

"Now get going now and enjoy your time as kids because trust me you will miss it when your adults." Mark said, the teens left the history block and went sit on one of the many grass verges in the academy. They watched as their classmates chatted and laughed and played together, unaware of what they missed.

"I'm glad it's all over now," said Sophie.

Last to survive

"Yeah, things can go back to normal." Andrew said before taking a bite from his sandwich,

"Well as normal as it was before," said Jake. They all laughed. The teens then carried on with their lives, with the peaceful thought in their mind that Ubel will never bother them or anyone else again.

So, there you go, four ordinary school kids beat a powerful yet evil sorcerer, it just goes to show that you can do anything if your friendship is strong enough. Hopefully it doesn't involve anything as dangerous as what our teens have done. But will they need to use their powers again? Only time will tell.

The end.

Printed in Poland
by Amazon Fulfillment
Poland Sp. z o.o., Wrocław